Essential Activities for Leveled Books

TABLE OF CONTENTS

Comprehension Strategy	Explanation
Analyze character	Use clues and evidence in the text (character descriptions, dialogue, actions, thoughts) to make inferences about the characters in a text.
Analyze story elements	Examine the literary elements in a story—its characters, setting, and plot—to develop an appreciation and understanding of the work.
Analyze text structure and organization	Use signal words and other clues and evidence to identify how and why the author wrote the text.
Compare and contrast	Find ways that two things are alike and different.
Draw conclusions	Determine what the author is suggesting without directly stating it. Conclusions are made during and after reading, and they are made from multiple (3+) pieces of information from the text. Students' conclusions will vary but must be drawn from the evidence in the text and background knowledge.
Evaluate author's purpose	Determine why the author wrote the passage or included specific information or text and graphic features. Authors can have more than one purpose for writing a text. These purposes may include to entertain, to inform, and to persuade. In addition, authors may have many reasons for including specific features in a text—for example, to clarify information, develop characters, and make a reader think.
Identify cause and effect	Find things that happened (effect) and why they happened (cause). A text may contain multiple causes and effects.
Identify main idea and supporting details	Determine what the paragraph, page, or chapter is mostly about. Sometimes the main idea is stated and sometimes it is implied. Students must choose details that support the main idea, not just any detail.
Identify sequence of events	Determine order of events for topics such as history, science, or biography.
Make inferences	Determine what the author is suggesting without directly stating it. Inferences are usually made during reading and are made using one or two pieces of information from the text. Students' inferences will vary but must be made from the evidence in the text and their own background knowledge.
Make predictions	Determine what might happen next in a story or nonfiction piece. Predictions are based on information presented in the text.
Summarize information	Take key ideas from the text and put them together to create a shorter version of the original text. Summaries should have few, if any, details.

Model Lesson for Leveled Books

Small-group reading is an assisted literacy experience in which the teacher supports and guides students with texts on their instructional level before, during, and after reading. Each small group consists of two to six students. The flexible setting allows the teacher to match students' reading abilities to appropriate materials, to observe reading behaviors, and to model and prompt for specific strategies that will improve students' word solving, comprehension, and fluency.

Planning

The small-group reading sequence begins by activating prior knowledge about the concepts, people, places, and objects that appear in the text that students will read. This is generally done before making direct reference to the book so that students approach the text already having connections to it.

The next crucial step is orienting students to the leveled text. Each member of the group is given his or her own copy. The students then locate the title and author, study the front cover illustration, and collaborate with the teacher in an introductory conversation about the book.

- For emergent to early students, the teacher provides a brief overview of the text and then prompts students to discuss the pictures and the author's intended message. The teacher incorporates structure by exposing the students to recurring language patterns and introduces visual or graphophonic cues by having students locate a known high-frequency word or predict the letter that they would expect to find at the beginning, middle, or end of a word.
- For fluent and advanced fluent students, the teacher provides a brief overview of the text and asks questions that prompt students to make predictions, such as: Will the book be fiction or nonfiction? What kinds of text features might be encountered in this text? What information might be presented? What might happen to the characters? What special vocabulary might the author use?

Both types of introductions prepare students to read the book by creating a supportive context for building meaning and providing an opportunity to discuss specific strategies that might be helpful during the reading, including using a related graphic organizer. The teacher then sets a purpose for the reading that may include a brief model of what the students' expectations will be during the first read.

Before Reading

- I'm going to read a nonfiction book, but I really don't know much about the topic. I think I should read slowly.
- I wonder why . . .
- I already know _____ about this topic.
- I've skimmed through the book. I know the word _____, but I don't know what _____ means.
- I saw _____ before when I went to . . .
- I skimmed through the book and saw lots of graphics and charts. I'll need to use those to help me understand what I'm about to read.
- I see some clue words or phrases that might help me figure out the text structure of this book.

During Reading

Students whisper-read or read silently, depending on their developmental level, as the teacher observes and monitors. To keep interruptions to a minimum, the teacher intervenes only when a student appears to be in jeopardy of losing the meaning of the text. The teacher then uses language prompts to help the student apply a specific problem-solving strategy at the point of difficulty.

Fluent and intermediate students may use self-stick notes to flag sections of the text that support their ideas about the author's purpose, to mark unfamiliar or confusing words, or to note information for the graphic organizer.

Monitoring During Reading

- When the author describes _____, I can picture it in my mind.
- I think _____ might happen next, because . . .
- This page was about . . .
- I need to remember _____, because it seems like an important point.
- Maybe I should reread this part and look for specific information.
- The graph (or other nonfiction text feature) on this page helps me understand . . .
- Since I don't understand this word, I may need to . . .
- This surprised me. I expected _____, because . . .
- Before I continue reading, I need to stop and think about what I just read and make sure I understand it. If I still don't understand, I need to make a plan.

After Reading

A short book may be read all the way through, while a longer book may be divided among two or more days. Students should be asked to reflect on the reading—both their use of specific strategies and their understanding of the content. Next, the teacher revisits the selection with one or two important teaching points that extend the students' learning to a higher level. These points are based on careful observations of the students' processing behaviors during the reading. The teacher uses the opportunity to validate successful techniques, activate strategies the students neglected or those with which they experienced difficulty, and focus on specific words, text or graphic features, literary elements, or other important components. Finally, the teacher builds comprehension by:

- having students retell all or parts of the text
- helping students make personal connections to the information or story
- asking concept and text-dependent questions and discussing students' responses
- helping students complete their graphic organizers
- helping students complete comprehension activities
- working with students to synthesize and assess the reading selection

Over the next few days, students are encouraged to reread all or parts of the text to strengthen the newly made connections, foster cognitive development, and promote fluency. In addition, the teacher uses the familiar text for additional mini-lessons, writing activities, and content connections.

Overview Analyzing Character

Directions for Activity Pages

- Hand out the first activity page, *All About You.*
- **Say:** *You are different from your family members and friends. Your family members and friends are different from one another. That is because every person has certain traits, or special features. Being kind is a trait. So is being bossy. Traits show up in the things we think, do, and say.*
- Together, read and discuss each trait on the page. Then invite students to put a check mark in front of the traits that describe themselves.
- **Say:** *Think of someone in your family or one of your friends. Put a check mark in front of the traits that tell about the other person. Do you share some of the same traits?*
- Explain that students can also analyze character traits or feelings when they read stories. Write the following on chart paper:

Analyzing Character

Find clues in the pictures.

Find clues in the words.

Think about what the character thinks, says, and does.

Think of words that describe the character or how the character feels.

Name ______________________________

All About You

Read and discuss each feeling. Then put a check mark next to the traits that describe you and your family member or friend.

Traits

Me	My Family Member or Friend
_______ kind	_______ kind
_______ bossy	_______ bossy
_______ patient	_______ patient
_______ cheerful	_______ cheerful
_______ friendly	_______ friendly
_______ clever	_______ clever
_______ quiet	_______ quiet
_______ fair	_______ fair

 Name ______________________________

Someone You Know

Draw a picture of someone you know well.
Then write three sentences about the person's traits.

_____________ is _____________ because ______________________________.

_____________ is _____________ because ______________________________.

_____________ is _____________ because ______________________________.

 Name ______________________________

The First Day of School

Read and discuss each feeling. Then put a check mark next to the feelings you and your classmates had on the first day of school.

Feelings

Me	My Classmates
_______ eager	_______ eager
_______ calm	_______ calm
_______ worried	_______ worried
_______ excited	_______ excited
_______ lonely	_______ lonely
_______ brave	_______ brave
_______ happy	_______ happy

Name ________________________________

How Do They Feel?

Look at each picture. Then complete the sentence.

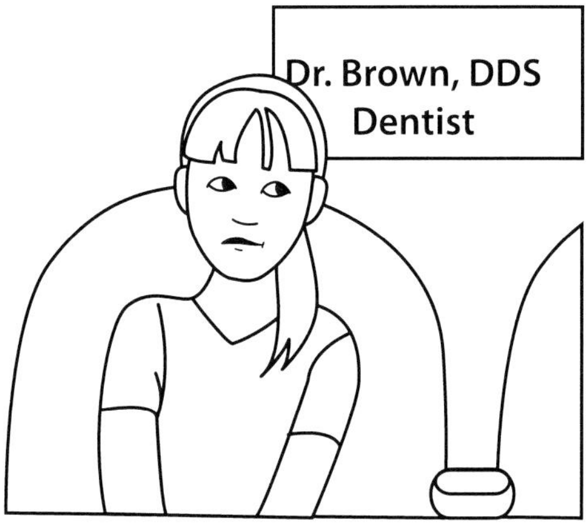

She feels ______________________________

because ______________________________.

He feels ______________________________

because ______________________________.

She feels ______________________________

because ______________________________.

Name ______________________________

Dear Diary

Read the diary entry. Write clues about Cassie. Then tell how she feels.

Dear Diary,

Today was the last day of school.

We spent the day in the park.

We ran races, played games, and had a picnic.

Our teachers played with us. It was fun.

At the end of the day, I said good-bye to my friends.

I almost started to cry. I'll miss them.

We're going to e-mail in the summer.

I hope they can come visit me, too.

Cassie

Clues	→	Feelings

Name ______________________ Date ______________________

Analyze Character

Character Name:

Clues		**Character Trait or Feeling**
	→	
	→	
	→	
	→	

Overview Analyzing Story Elements

Directions for Activity Pages

- Hand out the first activity page, *Name a Setting.*
- **Say:** *Today we will talk about setting. A setting is when and where something takes place. We are in a setting right now. I see the time on the clock. The time is a clue. I see clues in the room, too. I see my desk and the reading corner. I see books. I see you! These clues tell me that our setting is daytime in a classroom.*
- Invite students to look at the pictures and describe the settings they see. With a partner, invite them to tell a story that could happen in one of these settings.
- **Ask:** *What other settings can you think of? Remember that the place can be real or imaginary. The time can be now, in the past, or in the future.*
- Explain that they can also analyze settings when they read stories. Write the following on chart paper:

Analyzing Story Elements: Setting

Find clues in the pictures.

Find words that describe a place.

Find words that tell about a time.

Think about when and where an event could happen.

Name ______________________

Name a Setting

Look at the pictures. Label the pictures that show a setting.

bedroom	frame	library
pumpkin	soccer field	spaceship

____

____

____

____

____

____

Name ______________________________

The Setting

Read the passage.

Sunie closed the door and fell on her soft bed. The sun poured past the flowered curtains. Stuffed animals sat on the shelves. Her favorite books were piled on her desk.

Write the clues. Then name the setting.

Clues	→	Setting

Name ______________________________

In the Middle

Read the beginning and end of each story.
Then draw or write what could happen in the middle.

"I don't want to go to bed," said Ava.

Good night, Ava!

"I'm hungry," said Bear.

"Thank you, Squirrel!" said Bear.

 Name ______________________________

In the Middle

Look at the pictures. Draw or write what might happen in the middle of each plot.

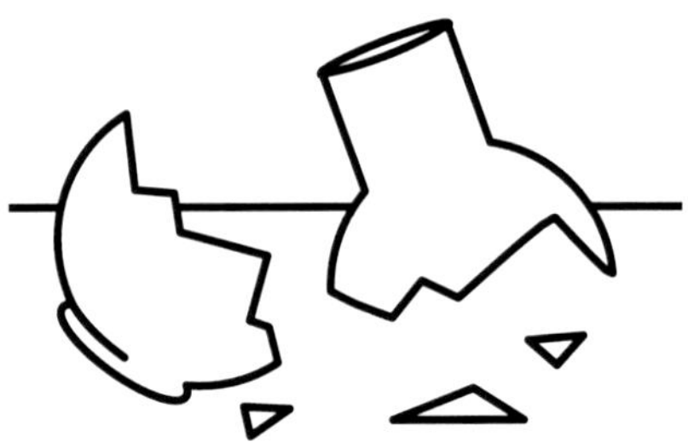

 Name ____________________

What Happened?

Read the story.

Reeba could not find her homework.

It was time for the bus!

She looked in her room.

She looked under the sofa.

She looked in the kitchen.

In walked Reeba's baby brother.

He had a paper in his hand.

"Look," he said with a smile.

Write what happened at the beginning, middle, and end of the story.

Beginning	Middle	End

Name ____________________ Date ____________________

Analyze Story Elements

Book	Setting	Plot (Problem/Solution)	Theme

Overview Analyzing Text Structure and Organization

Directions for Activity Pages

- Hand out the first activity page, *Sleeping Outdoors.*
- **Say:** *Last summer, I had a letter from a young friend. She was at sleepaway camp. She told me what she did every day. She told me about her new friends. She told me what it was like to sleep outdoors. She even told me how the food at the camp tasted. From these clues, I could tell my friend was describing her experiences at camp.*
- Ask students to read the description of sleeping outdoors on their page. Then ask them to draw a picture based on the description. Allow time for students to compare their drawings with their classmates' drawings.
- **Say:** *Description is one type of text structure we find when we read stories. We also find four other text structures.* Write the following on chart paper:

Analyzing Text Structure and Organization

Look for words that describe.

Look for words that compare and contrast.

Look for words that tell about cause and effect.

Look for words that tell about a sequence of events.

Look for words that tell about a problem and a solution.

Name ______________________________

Sleeping Outdoors

Read the description. Then draw a picture based on what you have read.

I lie in my cozy sleeping bag and look up.

A large branch creates a roof over my head.

Between the leaves, I see twinkling stars.

The moon is a glowing orange on a dark blue plate.

A gentle breeze blows across my face.

I hear the soft noises of the forest at night.

I feel the warmth of the campfire.

I can't imagine a nicer moment.

Can you?

Name ______________________________

Everyday Math

**Read the passage. Think about the evidence.
Then write the name of the text structure on the line.**

Word Bank	
Description	Cause and Effect
Sequence of Events	Problem and Solution
Compare and Contrast	

Long ago, people measured things with their feet and hands. As a result, their measurements were different. For example, one person's "two feet long" could be shorter than another person's "two feet long." Now that we have rulers, people can depend on one another's measurements.

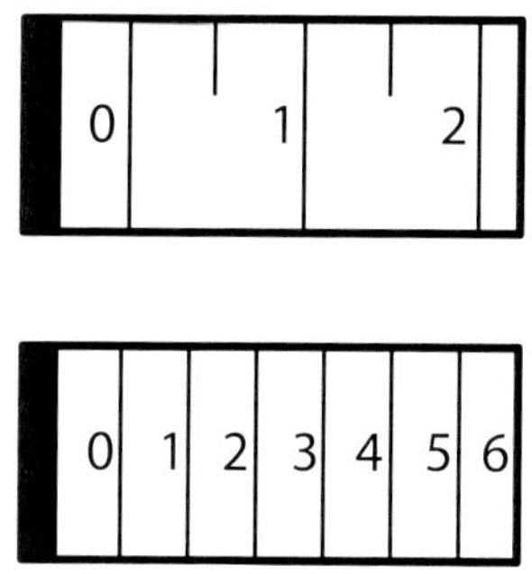

____

Name ______________________________

All Kinds of Weather

Read the passage. Look at the pictures.

Do you have different kinds of weather where you live?
Most people like sunny days best.
Some people like rainy days, too.
Lots of people like snowy days!

You can play outside on sunny days.
You can go bike riding and play ball at the park.
You can go to the beach or have a noisy
game in the backyard.

On rainy days, you stay indoors.
You can read books and watch movies.
You can play games at the kitchen table or on
the computer.

Some people stay indoors on snowy days.
Other people love to go outdoors and
build snowmen.
Which would you do?

This passage uses two structures. Think about the evidence. Then draw a circle around the correct text structures.

Text Structure:

Description
Sequence of Events
Compare and Contrast
Cause and Effect
Problem and Solution

Name ______________________

Community Workers

Read about community workers.

A community needs many workers to help it operate smoothly. Some people provide transportation. Some people keep the community safe. Some people care for people who are sick. Others build homes, sell food and clothing, or care for small children while their parents work. Every worker is important!

Description: Think of a community worker you have seen in action. Describe the person's job.

Sequence of Events: A teacher is a community worker. Tell how someone becomes a teacher.

Compare and Contrast: Think of two jobs you might like to have someday. Tell how the jobs are alike and different.

Cause and Effect: Sometimes a new business comes to a community. Tell how the business might change the community.

Problem and Solution: Sometimes a bad storm damages a community. Tell how the community workers can help.

Name ______________________

A Yard Sale

Read the sign. Write evidence from the sign. Then name the main text structure.

Evidence → **Text Structure**

Name ____________________ Date ____________________

Analyze Text Structure and Organization

Page	Problem	Solution

Overview Comparing and Contrasting

Directions for Activity Pages

- Hand out the first activity page, *Pizza!*
- **Say:** *Many people like to eat pizza.* Point to the first pizza. **Say:** *Look at the first pizza. Does this pizza have pepperoni? Yes!* Model how to draw a circle around the word **pepperoni**.
- Repeat the process with the mushrooms and olives, making sure students do not circle **olives**. Then repeat the process with the second pizza, making sure students do not circle **mushrooms**. Finally, invite students to complete the sentences to describe each pizza's shape and size (round; big or small).
- **Say:** *We can compare these two pizzas. How are the pizzas alike?* Allow time for students to discuss that both pizzas have pepperoni and both are round.
- **Say:** *We can contrast these two pizzas. How are the pizzas different?* Allow time for students to discuss that the first pizza is big and has mushrooms, but the second pizza is small and has olives.
- **Say:** *We can compare and contrast things when we read, too.* Write the following on chart paper:

Comparing and Contrasting

Look at the pictures.

Think about the words.

See how things are alike. Look for words like *alike*, *both*, and *too*.

See how things are different. Look for words like *different*, *one*, and *but*.

Name ______________________________

Pizza!

Discuss how the pizzas are alike and different.

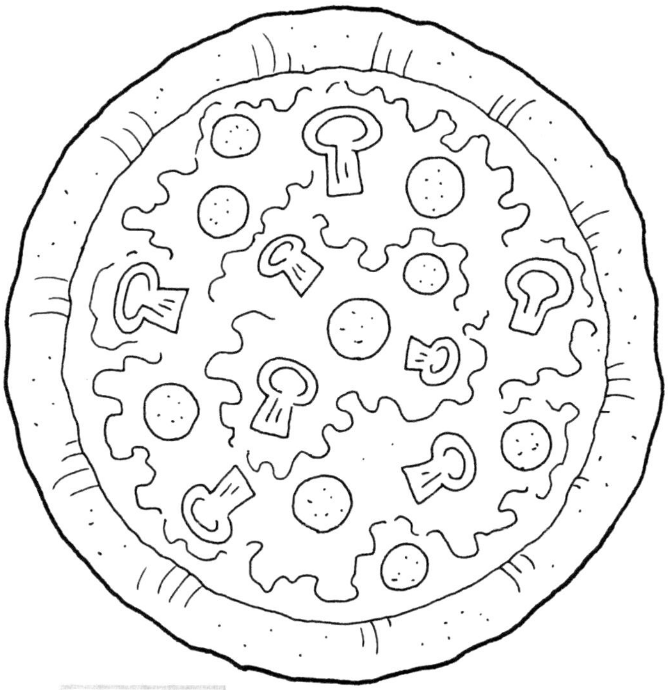

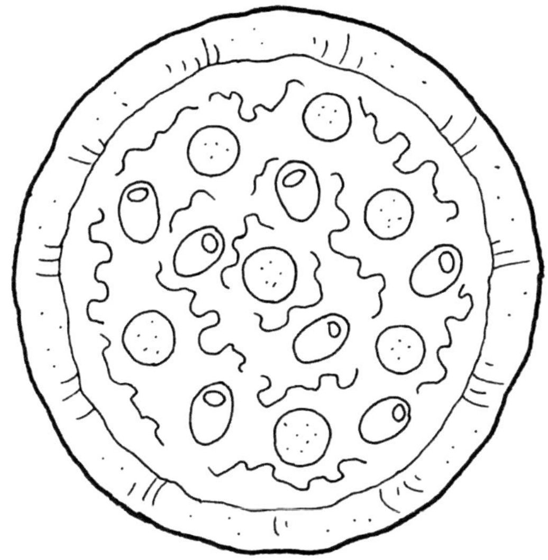

 pepperoni

 mushrooms

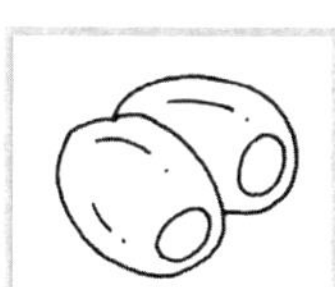 olives

 pepperoni

 mushrooms

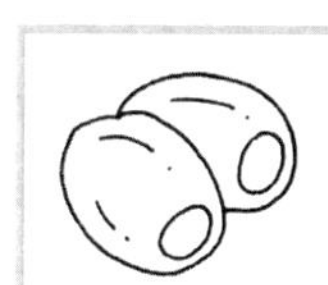 olives

Both pizzas are ______________________.

One pizza is ________________________ and
the other pizza is ______________________.

One pizza has ________________________ and
the other pizza has ______________________.

 Name ____________________

Patterns

Look at each picture. How are they alike? How are they different?

Draw two things that are alike and different. Tell a partner about them.

 Name ______________________

Two Planets

Read the passage. Then mark the chart.

Our solar system has eight planets. All the planets travel around the sun.

One planet in the solar system is Venus. Venus is a small planet. It has no moons.

Saturn is a planet in the solar system, too. But Saturn is a giant planet. It has rings around it. Saturn has lots of moons.

	Venus	Saturn
This planet is in the solar system.		
This planet has lots of moons.		
This planet is small.		
This planet travels around the sun.		
This planet has rings around it.		
This planet has no moons.		
This planet is giant.		

Name ______________________

Outdoors and Indoors

Read the passage.

Outdoor games are fun. Indoor games are fun, too. Baseball is an outdoor game. Go Fish is an indoor game. You need a yard or a field to play baseball. You can play Go Fish at the kitchen table. Both games have rules. Both games have a winner. What games do you like to play outdoors? What games do you like to play indoors?

Draw a circle around the best answer.

1. You need to play in a yard.	**baseball**	**Go Fish**	**both**
2. People play this game.	**baseball**	**Go Fish**	**both**
3. This game is fun.	**baseball**	**Go Fish**	**both**
4. You can play at a table.	**baseball**	**Go Fish**	**both**
5. This game has a winner.	**baseball**	**Go Fish**	**both**
6. This game has rules.	**baseball**	**Go Fish**	**both**

Name ________________________

Spring and Summer

Read the passage.

Spring and summer are both seasons. The air turns warm in the spring, but summers can be very hot.

Flowers bloom in the spring. Many flowers keep blooming all summer.

People go for walks in the spring. People go walking in the summer, too. People swim at the beach in the summer.

Write how spring and summer are alike and different.

Spring	Spring and Summer	Summer

Name ______________________ Date ______________________

Compare and Contrast

Alike	Different

Overview Drawing Conclusions

Directions for Activity Pages

- Hand out the first activity page, *What Is the Job?*
- **Say:** *Imagine you are looking at a person. She is at the wheel of a yellow bus. Kids are getting on the bus. She is smiling and greeting the kids by name. All these things you see are evidence. You can use the evidence to figure out that the woman is a school bus driver.*
- Tell students that using several pieces of evidence to figure something out is called drawing a conclusion. Ask them to draw a picture of another adult at work. Then help them fill in the evidence about the person's job. Ask students one at a time to read their evidence to the class. Once the class draws the correct conclusion about the job, invite the student to share the picture.
- Explain that students can also draw conclusions when they read. Write the following on chart paper:

Drawing Conclusions

Find evidence in the pictures.

Find evidence in the words.

Think about what makes sense based on the evidence.

 Name ______________________

What Is the Job?

Draw a picture of someone doing a job. Then list some evidence about the person's job.

Evidence:

1. This person ______________________.

2. This person ______________________.

3. This person ______________________.

 Name ______________________

What a Character!

Read about each character. Use the clues to draw a conclusion. Then draw a line to the right character.

1. I live in a castle.

   I have a large kingdom.

   My brother is a prince.

   We have a pet dragon.

2. I live in a forest.

   I can fly.

   I stay up at night.

   Animals come to me for help.

3. I live in an apartment.

   I'm a good big brother.

   I play soccer with my friends.

   I want to write a book someday.

Name ______________________________

Solids

Read the passage.

A solid has a shape.

A solid has a size.

You can see a solid.

You can touch a solid.

Your desk is a solid.

Your paper is a solid.

Is your pencil a solid?

What can you conclude about your pencil? Write your answer.

____

____

____

What evidence did you use? Draw a circle around the evidence in the passage.

Name ____________________

Frogs All Around

Read the passage.

Frogs live in most places on Earth.

They live on water and on land.

Frogs come in all sizes.

Some tree frogs are the size of a paper clip.

An African giant frog can weigh ten pounds!

Many people notice frogs when they jump.

One of the best jumpers is the common bullfrog.

What is one thing you can conclude about frogs?

____

____

____

Draw a line under the clues you used to draw your conclusion.

Name ______________________________

How Many Books?

Read the passage. Then draw a conclusion.

Sometimes we add.

Sometimes it is better to multiply.

Here are 5 books.

Each book has 10 pages.

Let's add.

10 pages + 10 pages + 10 pages + 10 pages + 10 pages = 50 pages.

Now, let's multiply.

5 books x 10 pages = 50 pages.

Which is faster?

Evidence	→	Conclusion

Name ______________________ Date ______________________

Draw Conclusions

Clues	→	Conclusion
	→	
	→	
	→	
	→	

Overview Evaluating Author's Purpose

Directions for Activity Pages

- Hand out the first activity page, *Movie Time*.
- **Say:** *My friend and I watched a movie on DVD. It was funny! The characters kept trying to get themselves out of trouble. The things they said and did made us laugh. From these clues, I could tell that the actors wanted to entertain the audience.*
- Ask students to Think/Pair/Share a DVD they think is entertaining. Then **say:** *Write the name of the DVD on your paper. Then draw a scene from the show. Be sure the scene shows why the DVD is so entertaining.* Allow time for students to share their scenes with the class.
- Explain that they can also evaluate an author's purpose when they read stories. Write the following on chart paper:

Evaluating Author's Purpose

Find clues in the pictures.

Find clues in the words.

Think like the author.

Think about how the author tries to entertain.

 Name ______________________

Movie Time

Think of a movie that is entertaining. Then draw a fun scene from the movie.

Title of movie: ______________________

 Name ______________________

Stories

Look at the blurb on the back of each book. Then draw a circle around the best answer to the question.

In this book, the author probably wants to:

entertain readers by telling a story from long ago

persuade readers to visit a castle

In this book, the author probably wants to:

inform readers how spaceships work

entertain readers with a funny story about aliens

Draw a picture that might be in one of the books.

 Name ______________________

Roll It Out

You can make your own clay. Read the directions.

1. Get one cup of salt.
2. Mix with two cups of flour.
3. Add $\frac{3}{4}$ cup of water.
4. Mix with your hands.
5. Roll out the dough.
6. Make something for a friend!

What is the author's main purpose? Draw a circle around the best answer.

The author is informing readers how to make clay.

The author is persuading readers to make things with clay.

The author is entertaining readers with a story about making a mess with flour and water.

Name ______________________________

Recycle and Reuse

Look at the blurb on the front of each brochure. Then draw a circle around the best answer to the question.

In this brochure, the author probably wants to:

inform readers where to recycle

persuade readers to recycle

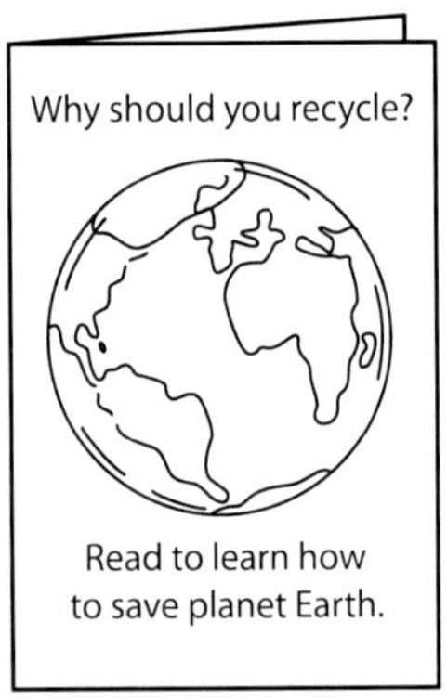

In this brochure, the author probably wants to:

inform people about the planets

persuade readers to recycle

In this brochure, the author probably wants to:

inform people how to reuse household items

persuade readers to recycle

Draw a picture that might be in one of the books.

Name ______________________

Healthy Foods

Read the directions.

1. Get two pieces of bread.
2. Put peanut butter on one piece.
3. Then slice a banana. Put the slices on top of the peanut butter.
4. Put the other piece of bread on top.
5. Cut the sandwich in half.
6. Share it with a friend!

What is the author's purpose? Draw a circle around the best answer.

The author is informing readers how to make a sandwich.

The author is persuading readers to eat a sandwich.

Name ______________________ Date ______________________

Evaluate Author's Purpose

Author's Choice	→	Why?
	→	
	→	
	→	
	→	

Overview Identifying Cause and Effect

Directions for Activity Pages

- Hand out the first activity page, *In the Yard.*
- **Say:** *My friend loves fresh vegetables. Because of this, she made a garden in her yard so she can grow her own vegetables. A cause is why something happens. What caused my friend to make a garden?* Allow time for students to respond. Then **say:** *An effect is what happens. What is the effect of my friend's love for fresh vegetables?*
- Write the words **cause** and **effect** on the board. Ask students to look at the pictures and write **cause** or **effect** under each picture as you discuss them.
- Explain that students can also find causes and effects when they read. Write the following on chart paper:

Identifying Cause and Effect

Think about what made something happen.

Think about what happened and why.

Look for words like *because* and *so.*

Name ______________________

In the Yard

Look at each row of pictures. Then label each picture *cause* or *effect*.

____

____

____

____

____

____

 Name ______________________

Two Squirrels

Read the story.

Leaves are falling. The air is cold. Winter is coming! The squirrels had a meeting.

"We must look for acorns," said one squirrel.

"Here is an acorn," said another squirrel. "And here are more acorns."

"If we hide a lot of acorns, we can eat all winter," said the first squirrel.

Write one of the causes and effects.

Cause	→	Effect

Name ______________________________

Drawing Shapes

Read the sentences. Look at the pictures.
Then draw or write an effect for each cause.

It is hard to draw a perfect circle, so many people . . .

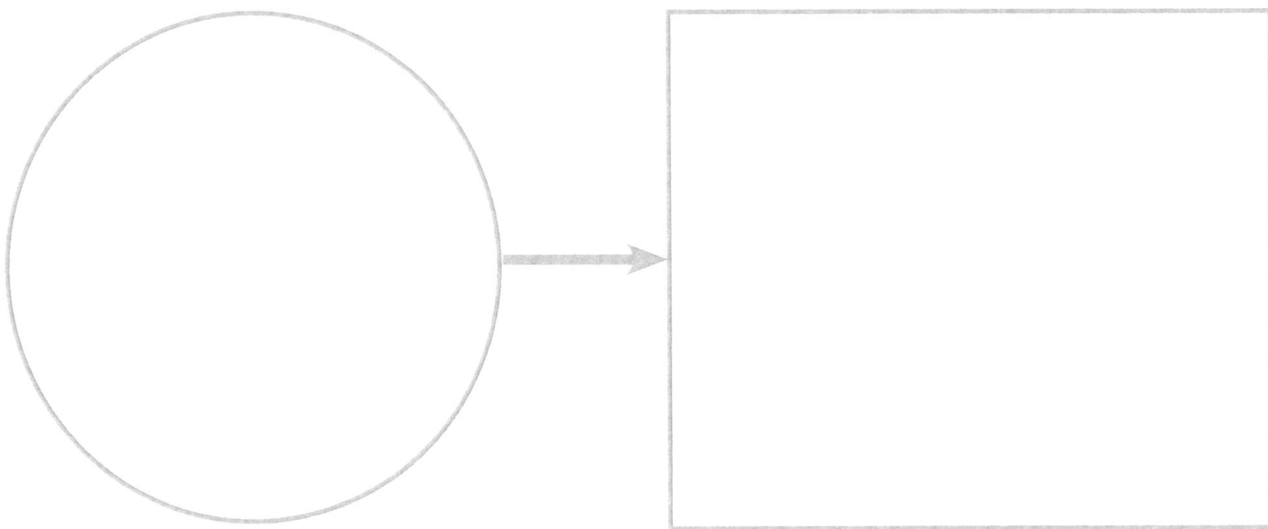

The sides of a square are the same length, so many people . . .

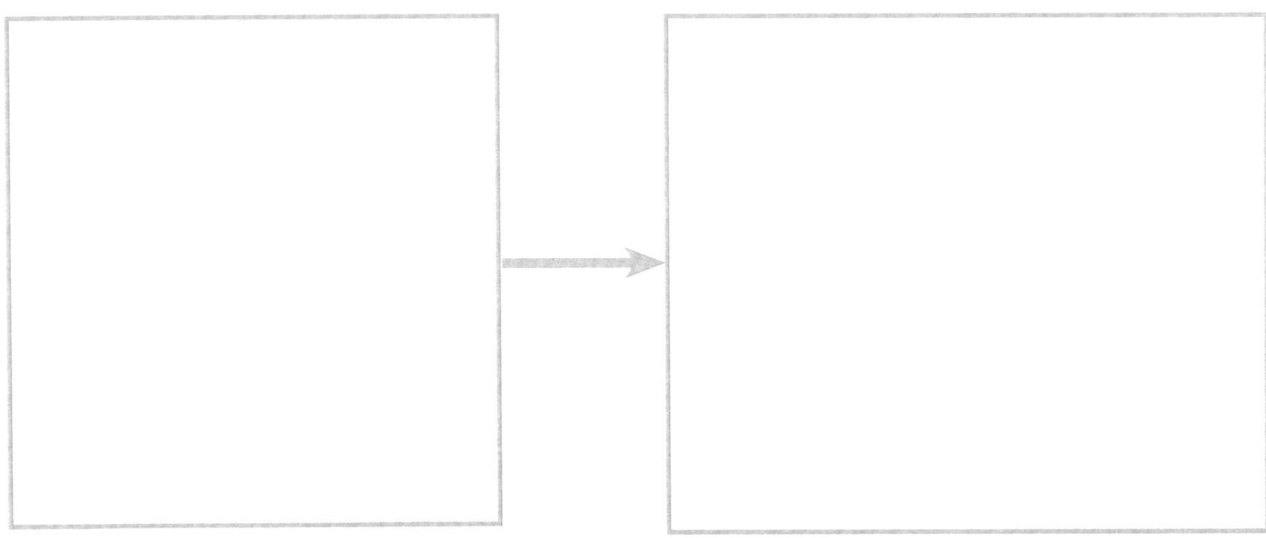

 Name ______________________

Why Do They Go?

Read the sentences. Look at the pictures. Then draw or write a cause for each effect.

People go to the library because . . .

People go to the laundromat because . . .

 Name ____________________

Spiderwebs

Read the passage.
Then write one of the causes and effects.

Spiders build webs. They live on their webs. A spider uses its web to stay safe. If something touches the web, the spider feels the web shake. Then the spider can run to a safe place.

Cause	→	Effect

Name ______________________________ Date ______________________________

Identify Cause and Effect

Page	Cause	Effect

Overview Identifying Main Idea and Supporting Details

Directions for Activity Pages

- Hand out the first activity page, *Our Class.*
- Display a class list on a whiteboard or projector screen. **Say:** *I will state a main idea about this list: We are a class. Find the main idea on your page. Draw a circle around the stated main idea.*
- Allow time for students to locate and circle the stated main idea.
- **Say:** *Now we will write some details that support the main idea. Look at the names of the people in our class. Write a name on each line.*
- Allow time for students to write a classmate's name on each line.
- Invite students to read their supporting details to a partner. Then explain that they can also find supporting details when they read. Write the following on chart paper:

Identifying Main Idea and Supporting Details

See what the passage is about.

Find the sentence that tells the most important idea or the details.

Find sentences that tell more information about the main idea.

Name ______________________

Our Class

Draw a circle around the main idea.

We are a class.

______________________ is in our class.

______________________ is in our class.

______________________ is in our class.

Name ______________________________

Stars

Read the passage. Draw a line under the stated main idea in each paragraph.

What is a star?
People used to think it was simply a tiny light in the night sky.
Now we know that a star is a giant ball of hot gas.

The sun is our closest star.
It looks bigger than all the other stars.
It only looks bigger because it is so close.

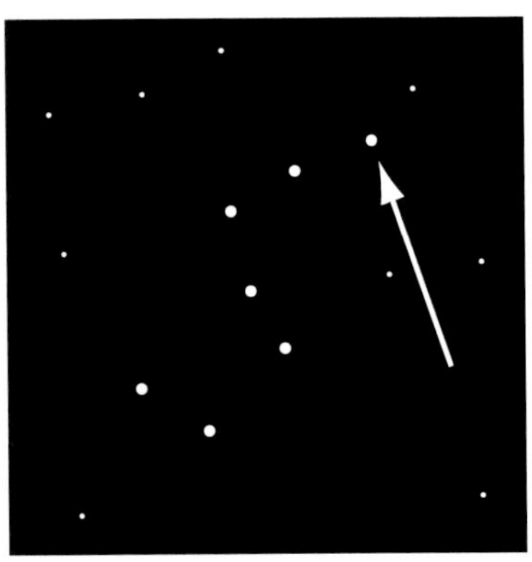

Have you heard of the North Star, or Polaris?
It is in a group of stars called the Little Dipper.
The North Star helps people find their way at night.

Name ______________________

Polar Bears

Read the passage.

A mother polar bear takes good care of her cubs. She digs a den to protect herself for the winter. In the spring, she comes out with new cubs. She stays with the cubs for two years. She keeps them warm. She teaches them how to live in their icy home.

Write the stated main idea in the first box. Then write the supporting details.

Stated Main Idea	Supporting Details

Name ______________________________

Picture Main Ideas

Look at each picture. Draw a circle around the best main idea.

The U.S. flag has stars.

The U.S. flag has stripes.

The U.S. flag has stars and stripes.

People can get many things at a library.

People can get books at a library.

People can get movies at a library.

Name ______________________________

Penguins

Read the paragraph. Find the underlined stated main idea. Then color in the circle in front of each supporting detail you read in the paragraph.

Penguins are birds, but they are swimming birds. Penguins are very good swimmers. They have wings that help them swim. They have webbed feet that help them swim, too. They can stand and walk on their feet.

❍ have webbed feet

❍ have fur to keep warm

❍ can walk

❍ have wings that help them swim

❍ swim everywhere they go

❍ are birds

Name ______________________ Date ______________________

Identify Main Idea and Supporting Details

Page	Main Idea	Supporting Details

Overview Identifying Sequence of Events

Directions for Activity Pages

- Hand out the first activity page, *Counting Coins.*
- **Say:** *Once I had some coins in a jar. First, I counted the dimes. Next, I counted the nickels. Then I counted the pennies. After that, I put the coins in my pocket. Finally, I used the coins to buy bread. Doing things in a certain order is called a sequence of events.*
- Remind students that the first coins you counted were dimes. Ask them to locate the dime on their page and write **1** in the box. Repeat the process with the nickel (**2**) and penny (**3**).
- **Say:** *Now look at the next row of pictures. Think about the story I just told. Put* ***1*** *on the picture that shows the coins before I counted them. Put* ***2*** *on the picture that shows what happened after I counted the coins. Put* ***3*** *on the picture that shows what happened last.*
- Discuss students' responses. Then explain that they can also find a sequence of events when they read. Write the following on chart paper:

> **Identifying Sequence of Events**
>
> **Find evidence in the pictures.**
>
> **Find words that tell about order, such as *first, then, next,* and *last.***
>
> **Think about the order in which things usually happen.**

 Name ______________________

Counting Coins

Listen to the example. Then number the pictures in the correct order.

nickel

dime

penny

Listen. Then number the pictures in the correct order.

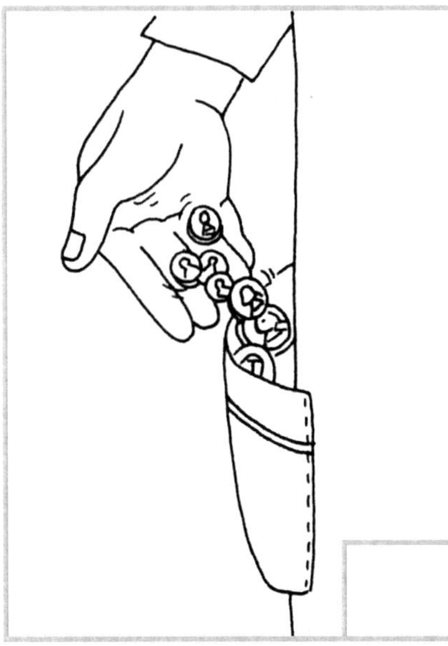

Name ______________________

Sledding

Read the story. Number the pictures to show the right order.

Jake woke up. He looked out the window. "Snow!" he shouted. "I'm going sledding!" said Jake.

"First, have breakfast," said Mom.

Jake ate some bacon, eggs, and toast.

Then Jake went to get his sled.

Jake put on his coat, boots, gloves, and hat.

Now Jake was ready to go sledding.

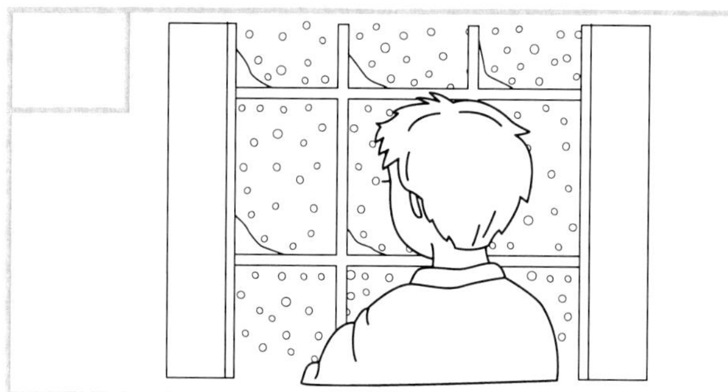

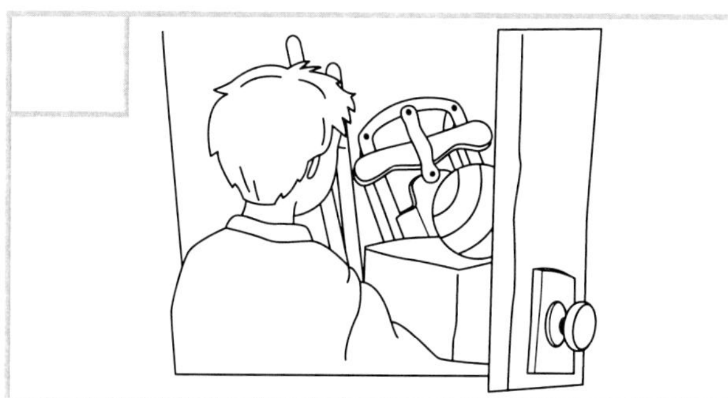

 Name ____________________

Old Paper, New Paper

Read the passage.

Old paper can become new paper.

Take old paper to a recycling center.
The old paper is sent to a mill.

First, a machine chops up the paper.

Then another machine mixes the paper with hot water.

Next, a third machine cleans the paper.

Now, the old paper is pulp.

People use the pulp to make new paper.

Number the sentences in the correct order.

_____ A machine mixes the paper with hot water.

_____ People make new paper with the pulp.

_____ The old paper is sent to a mill.

_____ A machine chops up the paper.

_____ The paper becomes pulp.

_____ A machine cleans the paper.

_____ People take old paper to a recycling center.

Name ____________________

Packing Up

Read the passage.

You are going on a picnic with a friend. Do you know how to pack a picnic basket? Dishes are heavy, so put them in first. Then put in the water or juice. Next, put in the sandwiches. Put the apples in last. Count how many things you pack in the basket.

Number the pictures in the correct order.

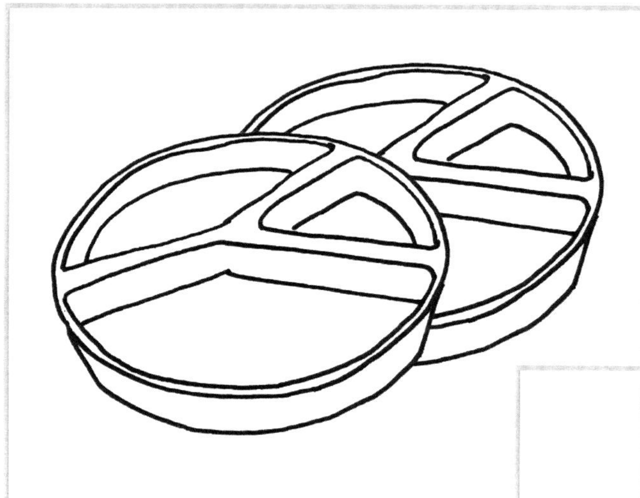

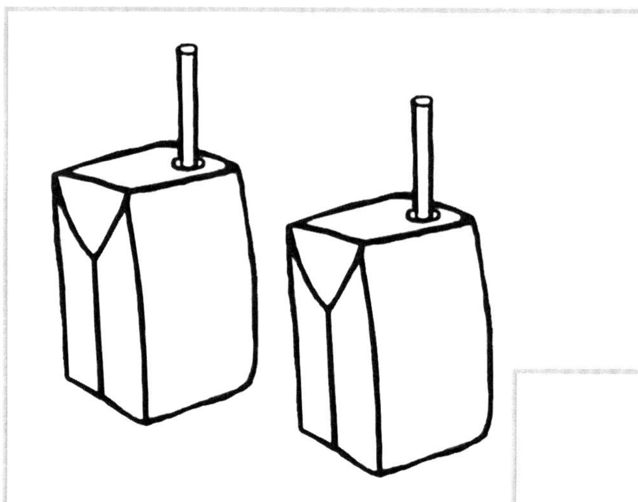

 Name ____________________

Jump Rope

Look at the pictures. What story can they tell? Then number the pictures in the correct order.

Name ______________________ Date ______________________

Identify Sequence of Events

Overview Making Inferences

Directions for Activity Pages

- Hand out the first activity page, *Where Are They Going?*
- **Say:** *Yesterday I saw a friend getting into her car. She was dressed nicely and carrying a briefcase. The clothing and briefcase are evidence. You already know something about dressing nicely and carrying a briefcase, too. Think about the evidence and what you already know. Can you make a good guess, or inference, about where my friend was going?*
- Allow time for students to discuss their ideas and then complete the sentence. They should infer that your friend was going to work. However, point out that an inference isn't always correct. For example, she may have been going to a job interview or meeting.
- Repeat the process with the other pictures on the page. Then explain that students can also make inferences when they read. Write the following on chart paper:

Making Inferences

Find evidence in the pictures.

Find evidence in the words.

Think about what you already know.

Try to figure out what the author does not state.

Name ______________________________

Where Are They Going?

Listen. Then make inferences for each picture.

The woman is going

______________________________.

The man is going

______________________________.

The kids are going

______________________________.

The kids are going

______________________________.

Name ___________________________

Picture Clues

Draw a circle around the best inference for each picture.

It is almost dinnertime.

It is time for bed.

The girl is going to school.

The girl is going to a birthday party.

The game is over.

It is time for the game to start.

Name ______________________________

Adding Up

Look at the picture. Then draw or write your ideas on the chart.

Evidence in the Picture	What I Already Know

Draw a circle around the best inference.

Teachers like to add.

The teacher will write *4* under the line.

 Name ______________________________

Duck Feet

Read the passage. Then write your ideas in the boxes. Draw a picture to go with your inference.

Ducks have feet that are wide and flat.

Feet like this are called webbed feet.

Webbed feet help ducks swim.

How can learning about duck feet

help people swim?

I know from the passage that . . .

I already know . . .

I can make an inference. People invented ______________________ after looking at duck feet.

Name ______________________________

State Quarters

Read the passage.

Did you know that every state in the United States has a special quarter?

The first state to have a quarter was Delaware.

This quarter came out in January 1999.

The last state to have a quarter was Hawaii.

This quarter came out in November 2008.

Write the evidence from the story. Write what you already know. Then write an inference.

Evidence

What I Already Know

Inference

Name ______________________ Date ______________________

Make Inferences

Page	Clues/Facts	Inference

Overview Making Predictions

Directions for Activity Pages

- Hand out the first activity page, *Tomorrow*.
- **Say:** *What day is tomorrow? What do you usually do at eight in the morning on that day? What do you predict you will do at eight tomorrow morning?*
- Allow time for students to draw or write their predictions beside the top clock.
- Repeat the process with the clock that says twelve (noon) and the clock that says five (in the afternoon).
- Invite students to share their predictions with a partner. Then explain that they can also make predictions when they read. Write the following on chart paper:

Making Predictions

Find evidence in the pictures.

Find evidence in the words.

Think about what usually happens.

Think about what you expect to happen and why.

Name ______________________

Tomorrow

Look at each clock. Then make predictions of what you will do tomorrow at that time.

Name ______________________________

What Is It About?

Look at the cover of this book. Draw a circle around the words that best complete each sentence. Then finish the sentences.

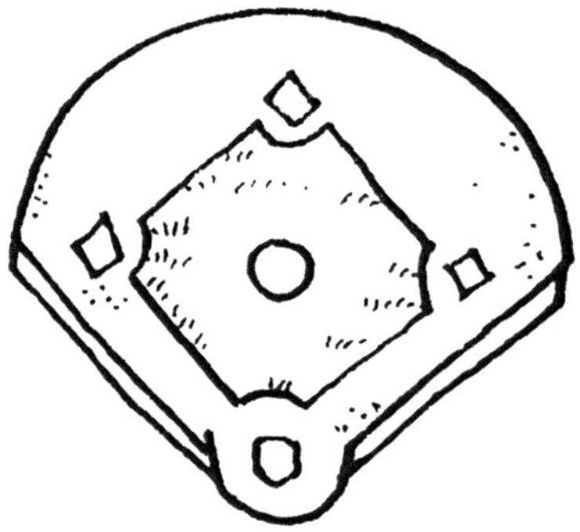

I predict that this picture (will be/will not be) in the book because

____.

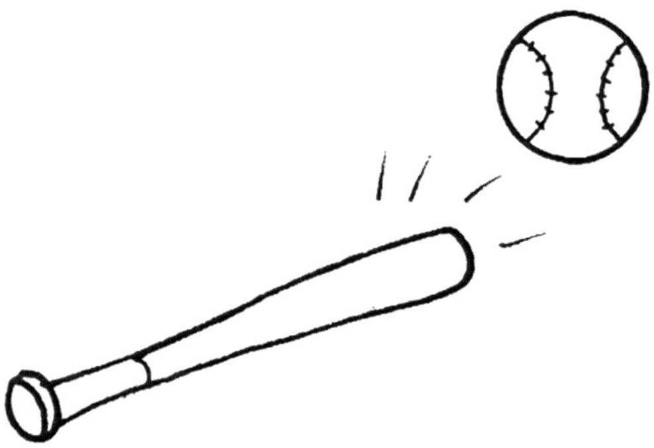

I predict that this picture (will be/will not be) in the book because

____.

I predict that this picture (will be/will not be) in the book because

____.

 Name ______________________________

The End

Read the sentences. Predict how you think the book will end. Draw a circle around the best answer.

All triangles have three sides and three angles. The sides and angles can be different sizes.

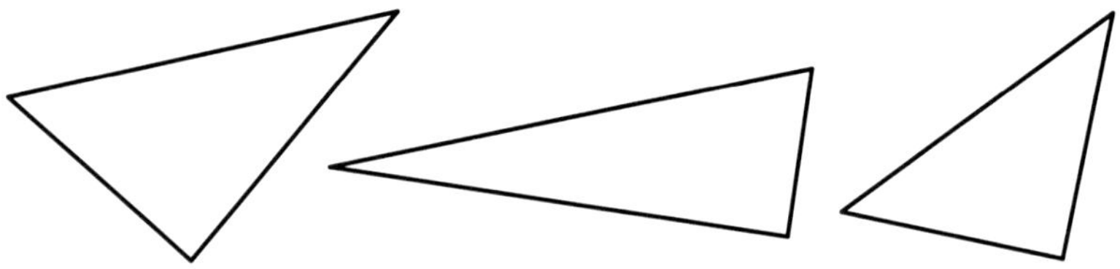

The author will . . .

- teach readers how to draw a circle
- show a picture made entirely of different types of triangles

---

Our solar system has eight planets. The planets travel around the sun.

The author will . . .

- show a chart summarizing what readers have learned about the eight planets
- ask readers if they would like to visit the moon someday

Name ______________________________

Doing Jobs at Home

Read the page. Then predict what you think will happen next in the book.

 Name ____________________

At the End

Read the sentence. Predict how you think the book will end. Draw a circle around the best answer.

Animals need many things. People can help animals.

The author will . . .

- ask readers to think of ways to help animals
- tell why dogs make the best pets

You can see cones all around. Some houses have a cone on top.

The author will . . .

- tell about some other types of houses
- show readers how to draw a cone

Do you send e-mails? Do you talk on the phone? You can communicate!

The author will . . .

- tell readers they should send more e-mails
- ask readers how people might communicate in the future

Name ______________________ Date ______________________

Make Predictions

Page	Question	Prediction	Clues/Evidence

Overview Summarizing Information

Directions for Activity Pages

- Hand out the first activity page, *New Baby.*
- **Say:** *Many people enjoy going to the library. What are some things people do at the library?* Allow time for students to respond, and then **say:** *I can tell about the library in one sentence:* ***People read, use computers, and learn new things at the library.*** *This sentence is a summary of things people do there.*
- Pair students, and ask them to summarize a trip to a place they enjoy.
- Then ask students to look at the pictures on the activity page and summarize the story. If they have difficulty, offer some suggestions, such as *A boy helped his mom take care of the new baby.*
- Explain that they can also summarize stories they read. Write the following on chart paper:

Summarizing Information

Think about what you read.

Pick out the big ideas.

Write one or two sentences about the big ideas.

Name ______________________________

New Baby

Look at the pictures. Then summarize the story.
Tell the story to a partner.

Name ______________________________

Fish Tag

Read the story. Draw a line under the big ideas.

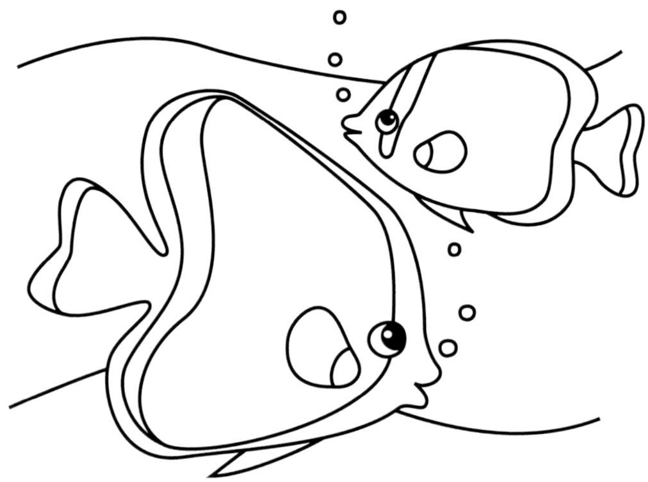

Two small fish, Fig and Swish, lived in the ocean.

They saw each other every day.

"Do you want to play tag?" Fig asked Swish.

"Sure!" said Swish. "You're it!" Swish swam away as fast as he could.

Suddenly, Fig saw a giant fish swimming after Swish. "Hide, Swish!" he called.

Swish hid behind a rock and beckoned Fig to join him.

A few minutes later, Fig peeked out. "He's gone—we're safe!" he said.

"That was a close one!" said Swish.

"We didn't get to play tag, did we?" asked Fig.

"No . . . but we got to play hide-and-seek!" replied Swish with a laugh.

Complete the sentence to write a summary.

Two ______________________ stay ______________________________

by ____.

Name ______________________________

It's Almost Time

Read the passage. Draw a line under the big ideas.

Telling time helps you plan.

The clock shows 12:45. Lunch is at 1:00.

The clock shows you how long you have to wait. It's almost time. Lunch is in 15 minutes!

Write the big ideas in the rectangles.
Write a summary in the circle.

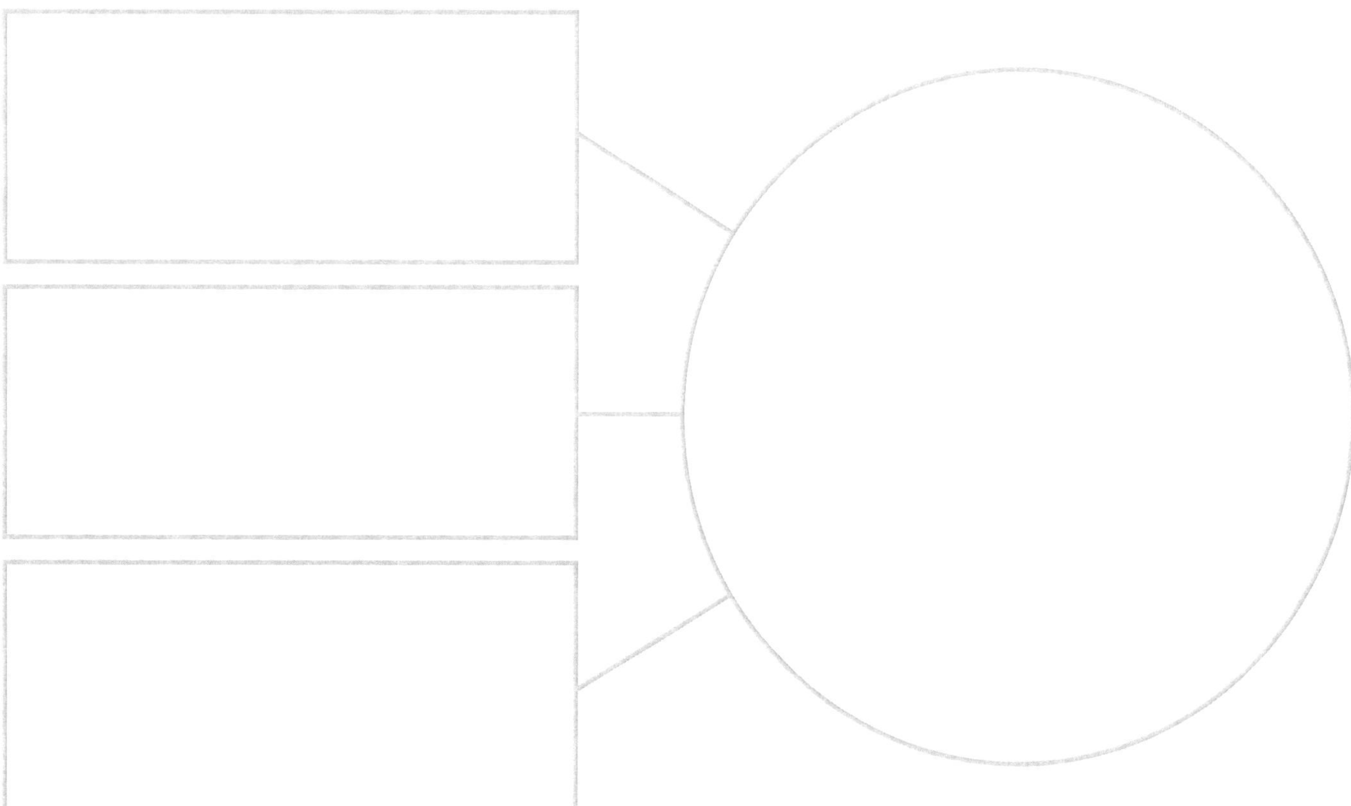

Name ____________________

Tornado

Read the passage.

A tornado begins over land.

It has strong winds.

The winds spin around in the shape of a funnel.

A tornado can hurt people.

If you see a tornado coming, find a shelter.

Stay there until the tornado is over.

Write the big ideas. Then write a summary.

Big Ideas	Summary

Name ______________________________

Cutting Shapes

Tell a partner about the pictures.

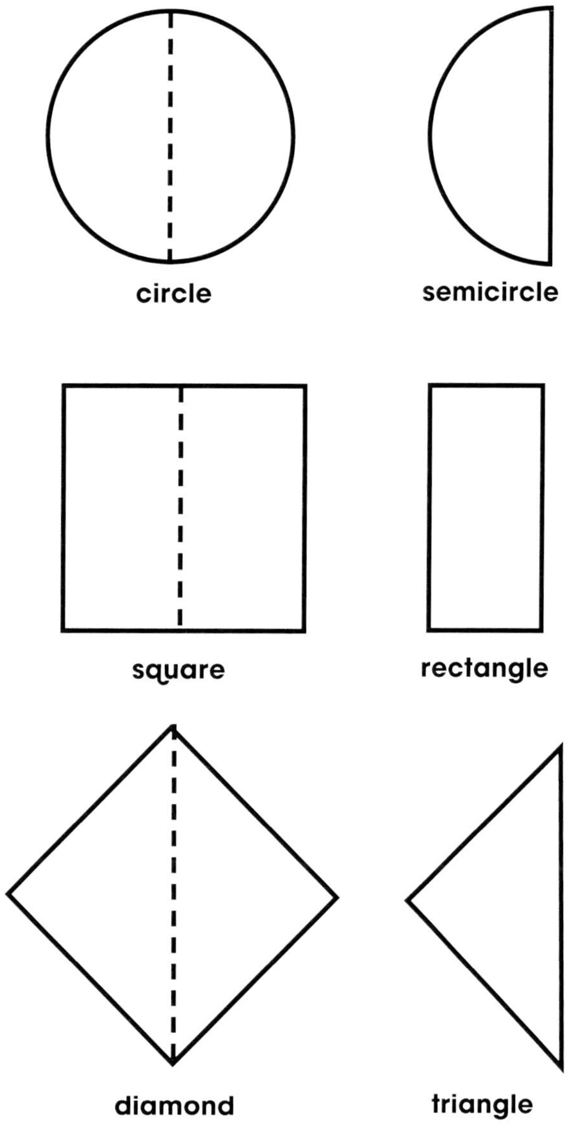

Draw a circle around the best summary.

When you cut a shape in half, you get the same shape.

When you cut a circle, square, or diamond in half, you get a new shape.

When you cut a semicircle, rectangle, or triangle in half, you get a new shape.

Name ______________________ Date ______________________

Summarize Information

Important Ideas	Summary

Conference Form

Student name ____

Book title ____

Author ____

Observations ____

____

Ask student to retell what he or she read.

____

____

Overall retelling ________strong ________average ________weak

Have student read a small portion aloud.

Notes on reading ____

____

____

____

Comprehension check ________strong ________average ________weak

Strategies used ____

____

Teaching point ____

Goal before next conference ____

____

Weekly Small-Group Reading Lesson Documentation Form

Teacher's name ____________ **School name** ____________ **Grade level** ________

Week of ________

Tier of Instruction

- Tier I: 4–6 students
- Tier II: 3–5 students
- Tier III: 1–3 students

Students' names:

	Lesson date: **Start/end time:**	**Lesson date:** **Start/end time:**	**Lesson date:** **Start/end time:**	**Lesson date:** **Start/end time:**	**Lesson date:** **Start/end time:**
Book title					
Book level					
Lesson instructional focus					
Lesson observations/notes					
Lesson follow-up/teaching points					
Needs to address in next lesson					
Other comments/ notes					

Weekly Small-Group Reading Lesson Grouping Form

Teacher's name ____________ **School name** ____________ **Grade level** _______

Week of _______

Tier of Instruction
- Tier I: 4–6 students
- Tier II: 3–5 students
- Tier III: 1–3 students

Small Group #1

Students' names	Instructional reading level (90-94%)	Independent reading level (95-100%)	Proficiency level: - Above grade level/advanced - On grade level/benchmark - Below grade level/at risk, strategic - Far below grade level/high risk, intensive

Small Group #2

Students' names	Instructional reading level (90-94%)	Independent reading level (95-100%)	Proficiency level: - Above grade level/advanced - On grade level/benchmark - Below grade level/at risk, strategic - Far below grade level/high risk, intensive

Small-Group Guided Reading Observation Record • Levels 1-4

Date ______________________

Text title ______________________

Text level ______________________

Chart coding legend

✔ reading behavior observed during lesson

Students' names	Reads fluently; problem solves on one or two things only	One-to-one matching	Directionality	Return sweep	Knows a small core of high-frequency words and can read them fluently	Self-monitors and attends to print, using high-frequency words	Aware of errors and searches the picture as well as the print	Rereads by returning to the beginning of the sentence	Cross-checks prediction at point of difficulty with the picture and print	Rereads at point of difficulty and articulates the first letter of the problem word

Comments/concerns

Small-Group Guided Reading Observation Record • Levels 5–8

Date ______________________________

Text title ______________________________

Text level ______________________________

Chart coding legend

✔ reading behavior observed during lesson

Students' names	Reads fluently; problem solves on one or two things only	Returns to reread closer to the point of difficulty	Beginning to search through a difficult word for additional information by blending letters into sounds	Fluently uses beginning chunks, or parts of words, and ending sounds	Meaning and structure are guiding the reading	Integrating meaning, structure, and visual cues; is moving toward automaticity	Self-monitoring, or checking on himself or herself; moving toward automaticity	Analyzes words using graphophonic patterns	Reads high-frequency words fluently	Recognizes errors when reading and initiates problem-solving actions

Comments/concerns

Small-Group Guided Reading Observation Record • Levels 9-16

Date ______________________

Text title ______________________

Text level ______________________

Chart coding legend

✔ reading behavior observed during lesson

Students' names	Reads fluently; problem solves on one or two things only	Problem solves at the point of error and makes multiple attempts to self-correct	Searches through the difficult word and blends sounds together	Takes words apart using large units or syllables	Meaning and structure guide the reading; uses visual information to check on reading	Reads longer texts with greater accuracy	Self-monitoring, or checking on himself or herself; moving toward automaticity	Uses word meaning and context clues to problem solve	Increasing control of visual patterns and flexible use of strategies	Reads high-frequency words fluently

Comments/concerns

____

____

____

____

____

____

____

Nonfiction Retelling Assessment

Use the following checklist during small-group reading to evaluate students' skill in retelling information from nonfiction texts. Record students' names in the first column. Then record specific observations, and/or mark **+** for **information given with prompts**, **✔** for **information given without prompts**, and **?** for **information not given**.

Students' names	**Explains the topic**	**Provides details to support the topic**	**Provides details in appropriate sequence**	**Utilizes appropriate text structures, such as compare/ contrast or cause/ effect**	**Explains how the topic has personal relevance**

Fiction Retelling Assessment

Use the following checklist during small-group reading to evaluate students' skill in retelling information from fiction texts. Record students' names in the first column. Then record specific observations, and/or mark **+** for **information given with prompts**, ✔ for **information given without prompts**, and **?** for **information not given**.

Students' names	Identifies the genre	Names the main character in the story	Identifies the story's setting	Describes plot details in sequential order, including the beginning, middle, and end	Explains how the story has personal relevance